D1077539

Knowsley Council

Knowsley Library Service

Please return this book on or
before the date shown below

1 5 JUN 2019

1 0 OCT 2019

Barrington Stoke

For Neil and Lizzy, with love

First published in 2019 in Great Britain by
Barrington Stoke Ltd
18 Walker Street, Edinburgh, EH3 7LP

www.barringtonstoke.co.uk

This story was first published in a different form as
Elaine, You're a Brat (Orchard Books, 1994)

Text © 1994 Oneta Malorie Blackman
Illustrations © 2019 Matt Robertson

The moral right of Oneta Malorie Blackman and
Matt Robertson to be identified as the author and illustrator
of this work has been asserted in accordance with the
Copyright, Designs and Patents Act, 1988

A CIP catalogue record for this book is available
from the British Library upon request

ISBN: 978-1-78112-824-4

Printed in China by Leo

CONTENTS

CHAPTER 1
I Don't Want To

Ellie glared out of the car window at her grandma's house. It was horrible. It was big and spooky and Ellie didn't want to stay there – no, she didn't! She sat back and started kicking and yelling. "I don't want to stay with Grandma," Ellie shouted. "I DON'T WANT TO!"

"But, Ellie, it's only for a few weeks," Ellie's dad pleaded. "You know I would take you with me if I could, but I can't."

"What seems to be the problem?" asked Grandma.

Ellie lifted her head at the sound of Grandma's voice. She didn't like Grandma. Grandma had black hair streaked with silver-white strands and wore a peach-coloured dress that was all ruffles and bows. She had old-fashioned spectacles in the shape of half-moons that perched low down on her nose. Her round, piercing brown eyes looked over the spectacles rather than through them.

"I won't stay with her, I won't," Ellie shouted. "She's dumpy and frumpy – and strict!"

"Ellie! That is no way to talk about your grandma," Dad said.

"Ellie, dear, you're just in time for dinner," Grandma said with a smile. "And it's all your favourites."

"My favourites have changed. You don't know what they are any more," said Ellie.

"Yes, I do," Grandma replied. "You like sausages and chips and baked beans followed by vanilla ice cream and chocolate sauce."

That was right! How had she guessed? "All right then," Ellie said at last. "I'll get out of the car, but only because I'm hungry."

"Wave goodbye to your father," Grandma said.

"I won't," Ellie said. "He won't take me with him."

Ellie walked towards the house and didn't look back at her dad once. Grandma watched Ellie and frowned.

Ellie's eyes were stinging from unshed tears. She felt so alone and miserable. Her dad was a manager for a large company that made computers, and he was always jetting off here, there and everywhere. Sometimes he took Ellie with him, but more often he didn't. Dad never seemed to spend longer than a few weeks in any one place.

As a result, Ellie had lived in more houses and been to more schools than she could remember. And because she had been to so many schools, Ellie didn't have any close friends. She hadn't been in one school long enough to make any. Ellie felt like an unwanted parcel, being shunted back and forth between teachers and boring aunts and even some of Dad's friends. None of them really wanted her.

"It's not fair," Ellie said as she kicked a stone along the front path of Grandma's house. Now her dad had dumped her on her grandma, who didn't want her. No one wanted her. There'd be no one to play with, nothing to see, nothing to do. Ellie would have to put up with tons and tons of nothing for a whole month until she started yet another new school in September.

"I hate school, I hate this house, I hate EVERYTHING," Ellie said as her eyes narrowed into thin slits and her lips turned down in a pout. Then she whispered to herself, "I wish … I wish I could find someone who wants to be friends with me."

"Come along, Ellie," Grandma said as she stood at the front door. "Before we have dinner, I'll show you around my home, as it's just been redecorated and a lot of things have changed."

Grandma took Ellie all around the huge house. Ellie was sullen in the basement, sulked in the living room, scowled in the bedrooms and sighed in the attic.

"I don't want to do this any more," Ellie said. "I want my dinner, please."

"Very well then," Grandma said, and off they went to the dining room. But Ellie missed Grandma's frown as Grandma followed her down the stairs.

CHAPTER 2

It's Been on the Floor!

The dining room was on the first floor, overlooking the back garden. The sun had almost set, so Grandma had to switch on the light. Ellie sat down for her dinner and she wasn't pleased. No, she wasn't!

"This sausage is too small," Ellie moaned. "The beans shouldn't be touching the chips – now the chips will be all soggy. And these beans are all clumped together. Yuk!"

"It tastes lovely," Grandma said as she tucked into her dinner. "Just try some."

Ellie glared down at her dinner plate. She took her fork and started stirring her food round and round. Soon it was one big blob on her plate.

"Don't play with your dinner, Ellie," Grandma said.

"I don't want these smelly beans," Ellie said.

"I'm sure they wouldn't want you, if you asked them," Grandma said calmly. "But you'll still have to eat them."

"And I don't want these stinky chips," Ellie sulked. "And I don't want this teeny-weeny rotten sausage."

Grandma bent down to tickle her black cat, Jolly, behind its ears. "Pretty Jolly, good Jolly," Grandma murmured. "You'd eat your dinner, wouldn't you?"

Ellie picked up her plate while Grandma wasn't looking. Could she do it ...? Should she do it ...?

"Jolly, I'm beginning to think Ellie is quite a young madam," Grandma said, still not looking up.

This will show Gran! thought Ellie. She lifted up Grandma's lace tablecloth and flung everything on her plate under the table.

"You're a good cat, aren't you, Jolly," Grandma said as she stroked Jolly's neck. "You wouldn't throw your food on my good carpet like some others I know."

Ellie stared in amazement at Grandma. How had Grandma known that Ellie had thrown her food on the floor? The lace tablecloth reached down to the carpet. Grandma couldn't have seen her ... could she?

"I'm not going to pick it up," Ellie said, and folded her arms across her chest.

Grandma sat up. "Pick what up, dear?" Grandma asked.

"My dinner."

"Pick it up from where, dear?" Grandma said.

"The floor!" Ellie replied.

"But your dinner isn't on the floor, dear," Grandma said. She prodded a chip with her fork and popped it in her mouth. "Look for yourself if you don't believe me."

Ellie looked down at her plate. It was empty. She bent over and lifted up the tablecloth. The sausage, the chips and every single baked bean had all vanished.

Ellie sat up again. "Well, it was …" Ellie stopped speaking as she stared down at her plate. The food was now back on it. Ellie blinked twice. She had to be seeing things. She lifted up the tablecloth and looked under it again. Then she looked back at the dinner table. The chips, the beans and the sausage were all back on her plate, arranged neatly.

"How … how did you do that?" Ellie asked. "I threw my dinner under the table." Ellie frowned at her plate. Grandma couldn't have picked up everything off the floor that fast.

"It doesn't matter. I'm still not eating it," Ellie said. "It's been on the floor."

Grandma looked at Ellie very carefully. "My dear," Grandma said at last, "I've met some bad-mannered, unpleasant characters in my time. Like that dreadful dragon who started living at the bottom of my garden and scared all the birds away. And that nasty, greedy troll who tried to eat me because I beat him at chess. But I have to say that you are the rudest, most disagreeable child I have ever met. In short, Ellie, you're a brat!"

"Does that mean you're sending me back home to Dad?" Ellie said hopefully.

"No, it does not," Grandma replied.

Grandma frowned down at Jolly and asked the cat, "Jolly, what should I do to teach this child a lesson?"

"Miaow! Miaow!" Jolly replied.

"Jolly is just an ugly, stupid cat," Ellie said, almost in tears. "She's as frumpy and dumpy as you are ..."

"That does it," Grandma said. "My girl, I'm going to teach you a lesson you'll never forget."

CHAPTER 3
Ellie the Cat

Ellie sprang out of her chair. She wasn't scared, not at all.

Grandma stood up slowly and pointed at Ellie. "As you think Jolly is so ugly and stupid, you will switch with her," Grandma said. "You will live in Jolly's body and Jolly will live in yours. And I won't change you back until … you find my wedding ring, which I lost years ago, and until you've learned some manners." Grandma's eyes gleamed.

"Don't talk wet!" Ellie laughed. But then something very odd happened. Lightning

flashed and thunder crashed *inside* the dining room. The room went dark. Ellie looked around, scared. Then the light came back on again and everything was still.

"There!" Grandma said. "It's done! How does it feel to be a girl, Jolly?"

Ellie stared up at the girl standing next to her. It was her!

She could see herself standing next to the dinner table, but how could it be her? How could she be watching herself? What was going on?

Ellie looked down at her hands. She stared so hard she thought her eyes might pop out of her head and plop onto the carpet. Her hands had gone. Instead she had … paws. Paws covered with thick black fur that shone like her hair did after washing it.

Ellie stretched around to look at her feet. More paws, covered in the same black fur! What was happening?

"Jump up on the cupboard and look in that mirror," Grandma said as she looked down at Ellie. "Then you'll see what you look like."

Ellie wondered why Grandma was so tall. Ellie began to walk over to the cupboard, but it felt so odd that she stopped. She was walking on all fours!

Ellie started walking again until she was just in front of the cupboard. The top of the cupboard looked very far away now. Before, it had been just a bit shorter than her head. Ellie looked up at it. She sat back and sprang up to the top, somehow knowing she could jump that high.

Ellie looked in the mirror on the wall in front of her. "I'm a cat!" Ellie yelled. Jolly's face stared back at her from the mirror. Only now it was *her* face.

"I said I'd switch you with Jolly. You're in her body and she's in yours," Grandma said, and walked up to Ellie. "If this doesn't teach you some manners, I don't know what will."

"You've turned me into a cat!" Ellie yelled again.

"I have not," said Grandma. "Like I said, you're just in Jolly's body, that's all. Your body's over here with Jolly in it."

Ellie the cat turned around and saw Jolly sitting at the table.

"Miaow! I love being a girrrrl!" Jolly said. She bent her head to lick at the baked beans on Ellie's plate.

"Jolly might be in your body, but she's still got cat habits," Grandma sighed. "Never mind. At least she can keep me company and she won't be as rude as you."

"I'm sorry, Grandma. Please change me back," Ellie pleaded. "I won't do it again."

"I can't change you back," Grandma said with a sigh. "Not until you find my wedding ring. What's more, you've only got until dinner time tomorrow to find it. I forgot that the switch-bodies spell has a time limit."

"But what happens if I don't find it?" Ellie asked.

"Then you'll have to remain a cat for ever."

"But, Grandma, please …" Ellie begged.

"It's your own fault." Grandma wagged a finger at Ellie. "You shouldn't have made me lose my temper. Now you'd better start searching for my wedding ring – unless, of course, you like being a cat."

No, Ellie didn't like being a cat – not at all. No, she didn't! She wanted to be a girl again. Ellie jumped down from the cupboard and ran out of the dining room. She'd find Grandma's ring if it was the last thing she did.

CHAPTER 4
Dimple Scrunchy

Ellie the cat ran along the landing. It was filled with low lights and long shadows. "I'm a cat," Ellie wailed. "I'm a cat!"

Ellie glanced down at her paws and wailed even louder. She didn't like being furry!

What am I going to do now? Ellie thought. She'd have to find Grandma's ring if she ever wanted to be a girl again.

Ellie was just about to turn the corner to go up the stairs, but she skidded to a halt. The huge shadow of some enormous beast was on the opposite wall. There was something around the corner waiting for Ellie ... It had towering legs and a long back and an even longer tail.

"Who ... who's there?" Ellie called out, feeling terrified.

A loud, deep voice from around the corner replied:

"My name is Dimple Scrunchy
I eat a rhino for my lunch-y,
I'm big and bad and bold and keen,
The meanest beast you've EVER seen!"

Ellie looked up and down the landing. She had to go around the corner. That was the only way to the attic, and that's where she wanted to start searching for Grandma's wedding ring.

Ellie stared at the long shadow on the wall. She couldn't sit there for ever, so she took a deep breath and called out, "I'm not afraid of you – whoever you are." Ellie's knees were knocking together so loudly, she almost couldn't hear herself. And now that she had four knees, they made a great deal more noise than two.

She walked slowly but steadily around the corner, holding her head high.

"Arrgh!" said a voice. "Jolly the giant! I've had it now."

Ellie looked down to where the voice was coming from. "Who are you?" she asked, surprised.

"Dimple Scrunchy the seventy-fifth – at your service!" said the mouse in front of Ellie.

"But you're a mouse!" Ellie said.

"Of course I'm a mouse," said Dimple. "Go on, Jolly the sneaky, get it over with. Don't play with me! Just knock my block off!" Dimple closed his eyes and stuck out his neck.

Ellie frowned. "Why on earth would I do that?" she asked.

Dimple opened his eyes and stared at her without saying a word.

"Was it you who made that giant shadow?" Ellie asked as she raised a paw to point at the wall.

"I did," Dimple said slowly. "I make the biggest, boldest shadow, don't you think?"

"Yes, I do," Ellie said. "It's very impressive, especially for a mouse. I thought you were at least as big as an elephant."

Dimple looked Ellie over. "Who are you?" he asked. "You look like Jolly the devious, but you don't sound like her. And you're not very smart, are you? Mind you, I've never met a cat who was smart. Sly, yes. Smart, no."

"I'm not a cat," Ellie said. "I'm a girl!"

"Does that mean you're not going to eat me?" Dimple asked hopefully.

"Ugh! Eat you? I don't think so!" Ellie shivered at the thought of eating a mouse.

Dimple breathed a sigh of relief. "Now I know you're not Jolly the sly," Dimple said. "She would have swallowed me in two seconds flat. So how did you come to look like Jolly the nasty?"

"Grandma put me in Jolly's body because I ..." Ellie began. "I threw my food on the floor." She felt very silly saying it.

"Why did you do that?" Dimple asked.

"I didn't want it." Ellie pouted.

"Why didn't you just say that you didn't want it?"

"Because I ..." Ellie started. She didn't really know why. "I ... just didn't."

"You're not very smart, are you?" Dimple said. "Are you sure you're not a cat?"

"My name is Ellie and I'm a girl, I promise," Ellie replied. "But I'll never be a girl again if I don't find Grandma's wedding ring by this time tomorrow."

"Where did your gran lose it?" Dimple asked.

"If she knew that, she'd know where to find it and then it wouldn't be lost!" Ellie said.

"Hhmm! Excuse me, I'm sure," Dimple said. "I was only trying to bloomin' help." Dimple tossed his head, turned and began to scamper off.

"No! Don't go," Ellie called. "I … I need your help. I'm sorry I was rude." Ellie wasn't used to saying sorry, but she thought she'd find the ring faster if Dimple helped her. And it would be nice to have someone to talk to while she was searching.

"Let me get this straight," Dimple said. "If you find the ring, then your gran will switch you back. You'll be a girl again and Jolly the folly will be a cat."

"That's right," Ellie said. "Please help me!"

Dimple frowned. "I'm not sure I want Jolly back."

"Does that mean you won't help me?" Ellie asked.

Dimple smiled and said, "Of course I'll help you. I'd do anything to get back at Jolly the horrid. I bet she just loves being a girl."

"That's exactly what she said before I left the room," Ellie said.

"That seals it," Dimple told Ellie. "I'll help you. Let's find your gran's ring!"

CHAPTER 5
Vinegar Blunderbob

"I was going to start in the attic," Ellie said. "Then work my way down to the basement."

"That's a bloomin' good idea," Dimple said.

So Ellie the cat and Dimple Scrunchy the mouse scampered up to the attic. It was dark and dingy and full of cobwebs. The only light came from the moon trying to shine in through the skylight above them.

Ellie padded through the open attic door. "It'll take all year to find Grandma's ring in this jumble," she said.

"Not if we have a plan," Dimple told Ellie. "I make the biggest, best plans in the world. Why don't we—"

"Please wipe your feet," said a squeaky voice. "What a distinct lack of manners you have."

"Who's there?" Ellie called out. She looked all around her to see who was speaking.

"PLEASE WIPE YOUR FEET!" The squeaky voice was much louder this time. "I go to a great deal of trouble and effort to keep this attic in tip-top, minty-flinty condition. You two just wander in here without—"

"All right, all right," Dimple interrupted. "Look, I'm wiping my four feet – see?"

"And I'm wiping my four feet," Ellie said as she wiped one paw after the other. "But I don't really see why. This attic is grubby and grimy and full of yucky-icky cobwebs ..."

"GRUBBY … GRIMY … CO … CO … COBWEBS!" the squeaky voice spluttered and squealed.

Ellie and Dimple heard the patter of lots of tiny feet heading right for them.

"What you so rudely call cobwebs are in fact the best silk tapestries!" the spider standing before them said. "Cobwebs are old and falling apart. If you bothered to look closely, you would see that each work of art in this attic is new. Each is woven with care and skill, patience and artistry, love and—"

"All right, all right," Dimple said. "We get the idea."

"Hhmm!" The spider folded four of her arms, still annoyed.

"I'm sorry," Ellie said. "We didn't mean to upset you."

"Cobwebs indeed!" the spider sniffed. "What nerve! What cheek!"

"I'm Ellie," Ellie said quickly. "I'm a girl, really, but my grandma switched me with Jolly the cat. So now Jolly is in my body and I'm in hers."

"I'm Vinegar," the spider said. "Vinegar Blunderbob."

"And I'm Dimple Scrunchy," the mouse said, and he bowed low. "I'm Ellie's friend."

"Are you?" Ellie asked, surprised. "Are you really my friend?"

"Of course I am," Dimple said with a smile. "I'm helping you, aren't I?"

Ellie grinned at him. "Thanks, Dimple," she said. "I've never had a real friend before."

"That's all very well, my dear, but we're wandering off the point," Vinegar told Ellie. "How long must you stay in the body of Jolly the detestable?"

"Until I find Grandma's ring," Ellie explained.

"Will you help us?" Dimple said. "Jolly the nasty loves being a girl. Right this minute she's having a good time while Ellie is stuck being a cat."

"That's why we're up here," Ellie said. "We're looking for Grandma's ring. If I don't find it by tomorrow dinner time, then I'll be a cat for ever and Jolly will be a girl."

"I much prefer you as a cat to Jolly the vile, if I may say so," Vinegar said.

"Thank you," Ellie said. "But I don't want to stay a cat. I want to be a girl again! Will ... will you help us?"

"Of course I'll help," Vinegar said. "I don't like Jolly the awful either. She'll be even more unbearable as a girl than she was as a cat. But first things first. I suggest our next step is to get some help for the search. Dimple, are some of your friends in the house?"

"One or two," Dimple replied.

"Will they help us?" Vinegar asked.

"If I ask them," Dimple said.

"And I'll ask my friends," Vinegar said. "That way we're more likely to find the ring sooner rather than later."

"It's … it's very kind of both of you," Ellie whispered. "I don't know what I would do without your help."

"Don't mention it, my dear, don't mention it," Vinegar said. "Anyone who doesn't care for Jolly the foul is a friend of mine. That cat is rude and disagreeable and never thinks of anyone but herself."

Ellie could feel her face burning. A lot of people thought that she was rude and disagreeable too.

"Let's both call our friends," Vinegar suggested. "After you, Dimple."

"Oh no! After you," Dimple said.

"Thank you. So kind. So polite," Vinegar said. Then she whistled three times – high, piercing whistles that made Ellie's ears tingle.

Almost right away, Ellie heard soft, scurrying, scuttling noises. Ellie looked around, surprised. It seemed as if the walls, the inside of the roof and the floor were moving in waves towards her. Then Ellie realised what it was.

Hundreds and thousands and millions of spiders.

"Um-hmm!" Vinegar cleared her throat for silence, then said, "Hello, friends. Ellie here needs our help to find her grandma's ring. She's been switched with Jolly the spiteful until she finds it. Will you all help?"

"But of course," one spider replied.

"Naturally," said another.

"Certainly," a third spider added.

The attic was filled with the noise of a trillion polite spiders all agreeing to help.

"Your turn, Dimple," Vinegar said.

"We'd better come out of the attic for this," Dimple said. "There isn't room in here for your friends and mine."

So Ellie, Dimple and Vinegar walked out of the attic, followed by a gazillion spiders. They reached the top of the steps that led down to the first floor and Dimple gave three low, long, loud whistles, making Ellie's ears jingle.

All of a sudden there came a rumbling and a tumbling and a pitter-pattering. The sound seemed to echo over the entire house. It

seemed to Ellie that every mouse in the world
was coming up the stairs.

"You lot took your bloomin' time!" Dimple
said. "Ellie here has got to stay in the body of
Jolly the hateful until she finds her grandma's
ring. She's only got until tomorrow dinner

time to do it! Are we going to help Ellie, or are we going to let Jolly the creep gloat over Ellie for ever?"

A lot of squeaks and squeals came from the stairs:

"No bloomin' fear ..."

"Never ..."

"We'll help you, Ellie ..."

"Thank you all," Ellie said, a lump in her throat at their kindness. "Between all of us we should be able to find Grandma's ring."

"Not so fast, my prrrretty one," came a voice from the bottom of the stairs. "I think you've forrrrgotten about me." It was Jolly, in Ellie's body.

CHAPTER 6

Help!

The mice screamed and ran, scampering up the stairs. The spiders fled up the walls behind Ellie.

"Have you come to help me too?" Ellie asked Jolly.

"You must be bloomin' joking, Ellie," Dimple snorted.

"My dear girl, surely you jest!" Vinegar said, and shook her head.

At the foot of the stairs, Jolly growled with laughter. "Me? Help you? I like being a girrrrl. I don't want to be a cat again."

"But that's *my* body," Ellie told Jolly.

"It's mine now," Jolly purred. "I'm going to make surrrre that I keep it."

"My friends and I won't let you," said Ellie.

"Yourrrr frrrriends?" Jolly laughed. "I'll show you what I think of yourrrr frrrriends."

Jolly dashed up the stairs after the mice. Her hand swooped down to catch the tail of the last mouse scampering away. Jolly lifted the mouse over her mouth and dangled it there.

"Lad-luggens!" Dimple shouted out, running down the stairs.

"Yourrrr name is Lad-luggens, is it?" Jolly said to the mouse wriggling and jiggling in her grasp.

"Help! Help!" Lad-luggens squeaked.

"Well, Lad-luggens, you look like a tasty trrrreat," said Jolly as she licked her lips.

"You mean, evil, rotten cat!" Ellie shouted. "Put him down."

"I'm not a cat. I'm a girrrrl now," Jolly said. "But I think a mouse now and then would be a perrrrfect trrrreat."

Jolly opened her mouth to swallow Lad-luggens whole. Ellie and Dimple dashed down the stairs.

Dimple reached Jolly first, scampering over Jolly's shoe and up to her ankle. He bit hard into her skin.

"Ow!!!" Jolly yelled.

Jolly dropped Lad-luggens and looked down to see what was nipping at her.

Ellie caught Lad-luggens's tail in her mouth as he fell. She rushed up the stairs with him and let go of the mouse in the attic. Then Ellie turned and ran down the stairs to help Dimple.

Jolly was furious. She swiped at Dimple with her hands, but he darted between Jolly's feet.

"You leave Dimple alone!" Ellie said to Jolly, and threw herself at Jolly's skirt. "Run, Dimple, run!" Ellie shouted.

Jolly might have been a girl now, but she still spat and snarled like an angry cat.

Ellie let go of Jolly's skirt and dashed up the stairs after Dimple.

"Run, my prrrrecious, run," Jolly called after Ellie. "But it won't do you any good. You won't find yourrrr grrrrandma's rrrring. Even if you do, I won't let you give it to herrrr."

"You can't stop me," Ellie said from the top of the stairs.

"Can't I?" hissed Jolly. "We'll see about that, my prrrrretty." Jolly strode off.

Ellie, the mice and all the spiders watched Jolly leave, a confident smile on her face.

"Come on," said Dimple. "We have a ring to find."

Ellie, Dimple, Vinegar and their friends searched the house all night for the ring. They searched in the attic and they searched all the rooms on the first floor. Then they searched all the rooms on the ground floor and down in the basement. They found forgotten books and thrown-away hooks. They found a broken clock and a silver moon rock. They found a big blue box and some smelly socks. They found almost everything – except Grandma's ring.

The morning sun began to rise in the sky, and soon it was shining bright and warm. They all gathered together by the back door of the house, and Ellie knew from one look at their sad faces that the ring still hadn't been found. Just then, Ellie heard Grandma's light footsteps on the stairs above them. Ellie turned her head and saw her grandma, and behind her was Jolly.

Ellie stretched out her claws so she was ready if Jolly tried something else.

"Ellie, I'm glad you've found some friends to help you," Grandma said. She smiled as she looked around at all the mice and spiders.

"Oh, Grandma, please," Ellie pleaded. "You've got to change me back. We've searched and searched and we haven't been able to find the ring."

"Ellie, dear, I've already explained it to you," Grandma said. "You have to find my ring for the spell to be broken." Grandma took off her glasses to polish them. "I wish I could help you," she added. "I really do."

Ellie's heart fell all the way down to the end of her tail. But she couldn't give up. The ring had to be somewhere. Maybe there was some place they had all missed? Ellie looked past Grandma and saw Jolly smirking at her.

Right! I'll soon get rid of that smile, Ellie thought.

"Grandma, there's something I've got to tell you about Jolly—" Ellie began.

"Ellie's going to tell you about how I offerrrred to help," Jolly interrupted. "I asked herrrr not to tell you, but I guess she thought you should know."

Grandma put her glasses back on and peered over them at Ellie.

"Now, Ellie," Grandma said, "why on earth shouldn't you tell me that Jolly offered to help you?" She turned to Jolly and said, "Well done, Jolly. That was lovely of you. If we all work together, we're bound to find it. And I'm glad to see you're all getting on so well."

Ellie stared at Jolly. Of all the lies Ellie had ever heard, that one was the biggest and the boldest. Ellie was speechless – and so were all her friends. They were glaring and staring and glowering and scowling at Jolly too.

"Well, I'll leave you all to it," Grandma said with a kind smile. "Don't forget, Ellie, you only have until dinner time to get my ring back to me. Good luck."

"Grandma, wait—" Ellie began, but it was too late. Grandma had gone back up the stairs.

Ellie stretched out her claws even further as she watched Jolly. "You lying toad!" Ellie hissed.

"Now, now," Jolly said, grinning. "Is that any way to talk to the cat who's now got yourrrr body?"

"Not for much longer," Ellie replied.

"But you've searrrrched the whole house and you haven't found the rrrring," Jolly said. "And if it has anything to do with me, you neverrrr will." Jolly's smile disappeared and was replaced with a nasty sneer. With that, Jolly bounded up the stairs without looking back.

Ellie watched Jolly go. She wanted to shout out to Jolly that they would find the ring – no problem. But the whole house had been searched now and they'd found ... nothing.

"I'm going to be a cat for ever," Ellie said slowly. She lay down with her head on her front paws.

"Nonsense, dear," Vinegar said. "You're not going to let Jolly the dreadful beat you, are you?"

"But we haven't found the ring," Ellie pointed out. "And there's nowhere else left to search." Ellie, all the mice and all the spiders sat in silence, wondering what they could do next.

CHAPTER 7
We'll Never Find It

"I've got it," Vinegar said. Her voice was so unexpected, it made everyone jump. "There's still one place we haven't explored yet," Vinegar explained. "We haven't searched the garden."

"The garden!" Dimple said. "I forgot all about that."

Ellie sat up. "The garden?" she asked. "But the garden is huge."

"So what?" Dimple said. "There are plenty of us here. We'll all stretch out in a line and walk from one end of the garden to the other to look for the ring."

"There's a well and lots of trees in the garden," Vinegar said. "We can search those as well."

"Why do we need to search the trees?" Ellie asked. "Grandma's ring won't be up in one of those!"

"You never know, dear," Vinegar said.

"A bird may have carried the ring up and put it on a twig for all we know," Dimple said.

So out they all went into the garden. The mice and spiders lined up along the outside wall of the house, standing foot to foot to foot to foot. More mice and spiders stood in a line in front of the first row and another row lined up ahead of that. It meant that if the first line missed the ring, then the second line would not, and even if they did, the third line was bound to spot it.

"OK, friends, stay alert," Vinegar ordered.

"Keep your eyes peeled, everyone," Dimple piped up.

Slowly, oh so slowly, the lines of mice and spiders inched their way forward. The sun was high in the sky before they had even covered half of the garden. And the sun had begun to lower very, very slowly down again before they had got three-quarters of the way.

Ellie looked up at the sky, then up at her grandma's dining-room window. She had less than an hour left to find the ring, otherwise she was going to be a cat for ever. There was still a patch of garden left to search, but a few mice and spiders were beginning to mumble and grumble.

"We'll never find this ring ..."

"This is silly ..."

"It's a total waste of time ..."

Ellie hung her head. She understood that those mice and spiders would rather be doing something else. It wasn't much fun, sniffing and scratching at the grass and ground to try to find Grandma's ring. Ellie's neck and her eyeballs ached from peering at the ground. Ellie was sure that everyone was as tired as she was. After all, none of them had got any sleep.

"Listen, everyone," Ellie called out. "I ... I know that some of you are getting fed up. You ... you can go if you want to. But I still want to thank you for helping me ..."

Vinegar scampered up the wall of the well to stand at the top of it. "Friends, we can't leave Ellie in her hour of need," Vinegar cried. "Ellie is our friend – we can't let her down. And besides, do you want to see Jolly the revolting stay as a girl in Ellie's body? Is it right that Ellie should be a cat for the rest of her life? No! NO!"

"Come on, mates," Dimple shouted. "Vinegar's right. Ellie needs us. Are we going to let her down?"

"No!" everyone shouted.

"Hooray!" Vinegar yelled. She jumped up and down on top of the well, waving all of her arms and legs. But she jumped up a bit too high and waved her eight arms and legs a bit too hard.

SPLOSH! Vinegar fell backwards into the well.

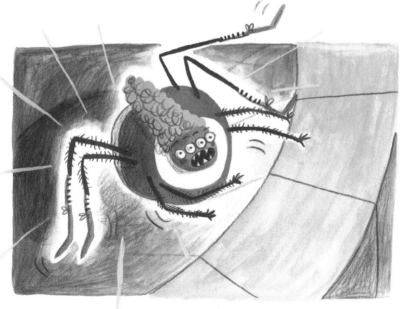

"Vinegar!" Ellie shouted. She jumped up onto the wall of the well and peered down into the shadowy water below. "Vinegar, are you all right?"

"Oh dear!" Vinegar called back up. "What a state! I'm soaked. Yes, dear, I'm all right. But I can't believe I was so clumsy. I'm not normally like that. And the fresh silk I spun just this morning is ruined!"

"How are we going to get you out?" Ellie called down.

"I'll climb out," Vinegar said.

Vinegar placed her arms and legs on the walls of the well, but they just slipped off. She tried again, but the same thing happened.

"Oh dear, the walls are slippery and slimy," Vinegar said.

"Can't you climb up?" Ellie asked.

"I can't get a foothold, dear," Vinegar replied. "I'm going to have to tread water for a while."

"But if we leave you down there, you'll get tired," Ellie said. "Then you'll sink into the water and drown!"

"Never mind that. Leave me here," Vinegar ordered. "You can't waste time helping me. You need to find the ring."

"But we can't leave you," Ellie said.

"You're going to have to decide what we should do, Ellie," Dimple said. "Whatever you think is best."

"Ellie, go!" Vinegar ordered. "If you try to save me, by the time you fish me out it will be dinner time. If you help me, you'll be a cat for ever."

CHAPTER 8
A Decision to Make

Ellie looked at the mice and spiders. They were all watching her, waiting to hear what she would decide. Ellie thought hard. They didn't have time to search for the ring and to rescue Vinegar. They'd have to do one or the other. If they searched for Grandma's ring, Vinegar would drown. But if they rescued Vinegar, then Ellie would be a cat for the rest of her life.

Ellie looked at Dimple and all the other mice. She looked at all the spiders who were helping her because Vinegar had asked them to. They were her friends. She'd never had any friends that liked her and helped her before.

When she'd been a girl, she'd been really selfish and only thought about herself.

"Vinegar, hang on," Ellie shouted. "We're going to get you out."

The garden was filled with the sound of all the mice and spiders cheering.

"Yippee!"

"Hooray!"

"Listen, everyone!" Ellie shouted. "We'll need some spiders to form a ladder down the well. Then Vinegar can climb up on their backs. The spiders at the top of the well can hold on to a chain of mice to make sure they don't slip."

The spiders began slowly but surely climbing over each other. They held on to each other's arms and legs as they made a ladder down the well. Progress was steady but very slow.

"Ellie, dear, I'm so sorry," Vinegar called out. "If I hadn't been so clumsy, then you wouldn't have to do this."

"Don't be silly," Ellie called down into the well. Her voice echoed back at her. "We're not going to leave you down there. Besides, it's smelly."

Ellie wrinkled up her cat nose at the slick and slimy stink coming from the well. It smelled like a dustbin full of rotten food.

"I'm getting a cramp," Vinegar called out. "I'd better swim around for a while."

As Ellie watched, Vinegar began to swim round and round in circles. Then Vinegar screamed, "I've found it. I've found it!"

"Found what?" Ellie asked. She peered down into the darkness. "Vinegar, are you all right?"

"I've found the ring – your grandma's wedding ring," Vinegar yelled. "I've found it! It's jammed between two bricks in the wall here. I'll get it out."

"Be careful," Ellie called down.

At last, the ladder of spiders reached down to the water. Vinegar trampled over the other spiders' heads and made it to the top of the well. As Vinegar stepped out onto the wall, Ellie saw she had Grandma's ring dangling from her mouth. Vinegar dropped it on the grass by the well.

"Gosh, that was heavy," Vinegar said.

Then slowly and surely the ladder of spiders was pulled up by the chain of mice.

"We've done it!" Ellie cried. "We've done it!" Ellie beamed, licked up Grandma's ring and put it under her tongue. "Grandma will put me back in my proper body now."

"And not a moment too soon," Dimple said. "Look at the sun. It's so low in the sky. We've only got a few minutes."

"And none of you arrrre going anywherrrre," Jolly said from the back door.

"You can't stop us!" Dimple called out. "One of us will take the ring and get past you. You can't stop all of us."

"*I* can't stop all of you, but I have a few frrrriends with me," Jolly said with a sly smile. "Come out, my friends. I'm surrrre Ellie and the rrrrest would like to see you."

Cats and more cats appeared from behind Jolly until they filled the doorway. They climbed up the door frame, they covered the stairs behind Jolly, they stood ready at Jolly's feet.

"Let's see if any of you can get past me and all my frrrriends," Jolly said with a smirk.

CHAPTER 9
Jump!

"Why, you big bully, Jolly," Vinegar cried.

"You mean, vile and vicious—" Dimple began.

"Never mind that, Dimple," Ellie interrupted. "What are we going to do now?"

Ellie looked up at the sky. The sun was very low. Ellie could see Grandma sitting by her open window, just starting her dinner.

"Another ladder!" Dimple said. "We don't need to use the door. We can make another ladder of mice going up the wall to your grandma. Come on, everyone. We don't have a moment to lose."

"You'll neverrrr do it in time," Jolly said, and crossed her arms.

The mice ignored Jolly and clambered to make a ladder up the wall towards Grandma's window. Ellie watched, feeling worried. A row of mice stood under Grandma's window, then more mice got on top of them, then more mice got on top of them. The pyramid of mice grew quickly.

"Come on! Faster!" Dimple shouted.

The pyramid was halfway up the wall. The sun was getting lower. Ellie chewed her lip. What would happen?

"Quick, Ellie, start climbing," Dimple called out.

Ellie bounded up the pyramid, climbing higher and higher.

She had to be careful not to hurt the mice she was stepping on.

Jolly walked out into the garden to see what was happening. "Frrrriends, quick. I need your help," Jolly called. "Ellie is almost at herrrr grrrrandma's window."

The mice climbed faster to build the pyramid higher. Ellie was a metre away from her grandma's open window.

"Get them! Get them!" Jolly hissed. She tore at the pyramid of mice with her hands. The pyramid began to sway, then to rock, as Jolly pulled mice away from it.

Ellie looked up at her grandma's window. She was so near and yet so far.

"Jump, Ellie, jump," Dimple shouted.

"I can't jump that far!" Ellie called back.

"Ellie, dear, you can do it. JUMP!" Vinegar shouted. "The pyramid is about to fall."

Ellie sat back and then leaped at the window with her paws outstretched. She sailed through the air … She wasn't going to make it …

She grabbed for the windowsill, stretching out further than she'd thought she could.

She made it! Ellie used her back legs to push against the wall and jumped right onto Grandma's lap. Ellie spat out the ring just as Grandma put down her dessert spoon.

"My wedding ring!" Grandma said. "Oh, well done, Ellie, well done! I was hoping you'd find it, not because I wanted it back, but because I wanted *you* back. Mind you, you cut it rather fine, dear. Another five seconds and you would have been a cat for ever."

"Will you change me back now?" Ellie asked.

"Of course I will," Grandma said. "Jump down off my lap. As soon as your feet touch the carpet, you'll be a girl again."

Ellie jumped down. There was a flash of light and her body stretched and grew and she was a girl again. But she had no time to enjoy it. Immediately, she ran to the window.

"Grandma, please do something," Ellie said. "Jolly is hurting my friends! They helped me find your ring and now Jolly is mad at them because she wanted to stay a girl."

Grandma frowned as she got up and went to the window. The garden was full of cats chasing mice and spiders. Right in the middle of them was Jolly the cat, back in her proper body again.

"Jolly, what do you think you're doing?" Grandma called out.

All the cats froze – but only the cats. The mice and spiders dashed as far away from the cats as they could get. Jolly looked up at Grandma and yelped, "Miaow! Miaow!"

Ellie listened hard, but she couldn't understand what Jolly was saying any more.

"Don't lie to me, madam!" Grandma said to Jolly. "I see I have been fooled by you. You are not the cat I thought you were, Jolly."

"Miaow! Miaow! Mia-ow!" Jolly replied.

"I don't believe you," Grandma said. "Now, if you want to be welcomed back into this house, you will leave Ellie's friends alone. If you or your friends have hurt even one of them, then you can look for a new place to live."

"Mia-ow! Mia-ow!" Jolly cried.

Ellie wished she could still understand what Jolly was saying. Ellie watched as Jolly's friends slunk off, climbing up the garden fence and running away.

"I've never seen such bad behaviour," Grandma muttered. "I shall have to keep a very close eye on that cat in future."

Jolly kept her head bent as she walked past the crowds of mice and spiders and into the house.

Then the mice and spiders crowded below the window, filling the air with squeaks and scuttling sounds.

"Your friends are saying congratulations to you," Grandma told Ellie.

"I can't understand them any more," Ellie said sadly.

"Of course you can," Grandma replied. "Just listen with your heart, not your ears."

Ellie looked out of the window at her friends. She saw Dimple, and next to him was Vinegar.

"Thank you all," Ellie said, with tears of happiness in her eyes. "You were my first friends, and I'll never forget you. If Jolly ever tries to bully any of you, you must let me or my grandma know."

Ellie listened with her heart.

"Bye, Ellie," she heard Dimple shout.

"Goodbye, Ellie, dear," Vinegar said. "And good luck."

Then the mice and spiders scurried off across the garden in all directions until it was empty.

Ellie turned to her grandma. "Grandma, I'm sorry I was so rude to you," Ellie said.

"And I'm sorry I lost my temper," Grandma said. "Do you forgive me?"

Ellie nodded.

"Now then, I have some news for you," Grandma added. "Your dad went for an interview for a new job two weeks ago. Today he found out that he got it. He wanted to tell you himself, but you wouldn't give him a chance."

"What's his new job?" Ellie asked. She felt hope suddenly inside her, like a light being switched on. Ellie crossed her fingers hard – the hardest she had ever done in her life.

"He's going to be the manager in charge of selling and fixing computers in this area," Grandma explained. "So when he gets back, you and your dad are both going to live with me. We're all going to share this house – but only if you want to."

"Oh, Grandma ..." Ellie threw her arms around Grandma's neck.

"And that means you'll be able to go to the local school as well," Grandma said. "You'll be

able to make some real, lasting friends. There will be no more travelling – no more trips abroad, apart from holidays."

Ellie couldn't believe it. "Oh, Grandma, I'd love that more than anything," Ellie said with a grin. And Ellie and her grandma hugged each other tight.

Ellie couldn't stop smiling. She had friends now. Everything was going to be wonderful.

Our books are tested
for children and young people by
children and young people.

Thanks to everyone who consulted on
a manuscript for their time and effort in
helping us to make our books better
for our readers.